This book belongs to

....

❄ ANIMATED CLASSICS ❄

Disney

Frozen

Acknowledgments

Special thanks to the staff at the Walt Disney Animation Research Library and the Walt Disney Archives for their invaluable assistance and for providing the artwork for this book.

First published in the UK in 2019 by Studio Press Books,
an imprint of Bonnier Books UK,
The Plaza, 535 King's Road,
London, SW10 0SZ

studiopressbooks.co.uk
bonnierbooks.co.uk

Printed in China
2 4 6 8 10 9 7 5 3 1

All rights reserved
ISBN 978-1-78741-545-4

Text adapted by Lily Murray
Edited by Frankie Jones
Designed by Nia Williams
Cover designed by Rob Ward
Cover illustrated by Chellie Carroll

I have always loved fairy tales. They are my absolute favourite stories of all. They allow an artist the possibility to create environments and realms that are ethereal.

As a little girl, I would hurry to finish my assignments in class so I could daydream and draw. Soon Disney became a huge influence, and I began a journey that would lead me to work on my first animated fairy tales: *The Little Mermaid* and *Beauty and the Beast*.

When Chris Buck, Jennifer Lee and Mike Giaimo began working on *Frozen*, I ran to Mike's office and begged to be included. I knew that working with this team would be a dream come true, and I didn't want to miss out on helping bring this film to life. *Frozen* was a fairy tale like no other and set in the snow, which gave it limitless colour possibilities – a thrilling proposition for an artist. What's more, there was the ice, and the reflections that come from ice. I love sparkles, and I'm always being teased by my fellow artists about this love.

Working with Mike Giaimo is a treat. Not only is he a wonderful person, but he has incredible aesthetic taste in production design. A few years ago, when *Frozen 2* was announced, I once again ran to Mike's office and asked to be included. Like the first film, *Frozen 2* has a unique colour palette, this one showcasing the fall season. Mixing this warm new palette with the icy *Frozen* aesthetic pushed us to be creative. The two creative visions had to work together.

It's been an absolute joy to work on *Frozen* and *Frozen 2*. Both films have allowed me to use all that I've learned from my many years at the Walt Disney Animation Studios to help create a world where I love to play. And I've gotten to do it all side by side with people who make coming to work fun. There's nothing better.

From daydreaming and drawing to the big screen, the most important thing I've learned is that daydreams are as magical as fairy tales.

Lisa Keene

Walt Disney Animation Studios

*I*n the kingdom of Arendelle, nestled in a valley beneath moss-covered cliffs, stood a beautiful castle.

Inside, a young princess lay sleeping in her bed.

"Elsa! Pssst!" said her little sister, clambering onto the bed. "Elsa! Wake up! Wake up! Wake up!"

"Anna, go back to sleep," Elsa replied.

"I just can't," said Anna. "The sky is awake, so I'm awake. So we have to play."

"Go play by yourself," said Elsa.

For a moment, Anna looked defeated. Then her eyes lit up. "Do you want to build a snowman?" she asked.

At that, Elsa leaped out of bed and, hand in hand, the sisters raced down the castle stairs.

Giggling and laughing, they dashed into the grand ballroom.

"Do the magic!" pleaded Anna.

Elsa began rolling her hands, one over the other, until sparkling snowflakes appeared.

"Ready?" Elsa asked.

"Uh-huh," chuckled Anna.

Elsa created a glowing snowball that shot up to the ceiling where, like a fountain, it burst into hundreds of glowing snowflakes.

"This is amazing!" Anna cheered.

Next, Elsa made a snowman with coal-black eyes and a carrot for a nose.

"Hi, I'm Olaf,"
said Elsa, waving
his twig arms, "and
I like warm hugs."

"I love you, Olaf,"
said Anna, rushing
over to give him a
hug.

Then Anna ran,
jumping between
drifts of snow,
higher and
higher…

Each time she
jumped, Elsa
created new
snowdrifts to catch her, but Anna was too fast.

"Slow down!" cried Elsa. She stumbled backward, and in her panic,
she struck Anna with her magic.

Anna tumbled to the ground.

"Mama! Papa!" Elsa cried, holding Anna in her arms. A streak of white appeared in Anna's hair, and she lay motionless.

The ground around Elsa began to freeze. As her fear grew, the ice spread across the floor and up the walls.

"You're okay, Anna," Elsa sobbed. "I got you."

The door burst open and their parents hurried into the room. "Elsa, what have you done?" gasped the king. "This is getting out of hand."

"It was an accident," said Elsa.

"Oh!" said the queen, reaching down to touch Anna. "She's ice cold."

"I know where we have to go," said the king.

The royal family galloped away from the castle to a clearing ringed by moss-covered boulders. "Please! Help!" the king called out. "It's my daughter."

As he spoke, the boulders began to roll towards them. Then they sprang open, each boulder revealing itself to be a troll.

"Your Majesty," said Grand Pabbie, the troll leader, coming forward. "Born with the powers, or cursed?" he asked.

"Born," said her father, "and they're getting stronger."

Grand Pabbie touched Anna's ice-cold forehead. "You were lucky it wasn't her heart. The heart is not so easily changed. But the head can be persuaded."

"Do what you must," the king replied.

"I recommend we remove all magic. Even memories of magic, to be safe. But don't worry, I'll leave the fun," he said, touching Anna's forehead to remove her magical memories. "She will be okay," he promised.

"But she won't remember I have powers?" asked Elsa.

"It's for the best," replied her father.

"Listen to me, Elsa," said Grand Pabbie. "Your power will only grow. There is beauty in it, but also great danger. You must learn to control it. Fear will be your enemy."

"No! We'll protect her," said the king. "She can learn to control it. I'm sure."

From that moment on, the castle gates were locked. Elsa's parents were determined to keep her powers hidden from everyone, including Anna, until Elsa could learn to control them.

But as time passed, Elsa's powers grew. The king gave her a pair of white gloves to wear. "Conceal it. Don't feel it. Don't let it show," they recited together.

"I'm scared," Elsa told her parents one day. "It's getting stronger."

"Getting upset only makes it worse. Calm down," said her father, reaching out for her.

"No! Don't touch me," cried Elsa, backing away. "Please, I don't want to hurt you."

While Elsa kept to her room, Anna roamed through the castle, lonely without her sister. As the years passed, she no longer stopped to knock on Elsa's door. She knew her sister would not come out.

One day, the king and queen left the castle on a royal trip. But as they crossed the ocean, a powerful storm struck. Their ship was buried beneath the waves.

Anna had never felt more alone. She knocked on her sister's door. But there was no answer. On the other side of the door, in a room frosted with ice, Elsa sat on the floor, hiding her tears in her arms.

For three more years, the castle gates remained shut. Finally the day of Elsa's coronation came. People flocked from all over Arendelle and beyond to meet the new queen and her sister.

Elsa gazed out anxiously at the crowds. Today, she thought, looking at a portrait of her father, she must hide her powers.

Summoning her courage, she called out for the gates to be opened.

"It's coronation day!" cried Anna, overjoyed that there would finally be people in the castle. She ran outside, dancing through the warm summer streets. But when she reached the quayside, she walked smack into a horse.

"I'm so sorry," said the rider. "Are you hurt?"

"No, no, I'm okay," Anna stammered.

"Oh, thank goodness," he said. He dismounted, then extended his hand to help Anna up. "Prince Hans of the Southern Isles," he introduced himself, bowing.

"Princess Anna of Arendelle," Anna replied, gazing into his eyes.

"I'd like to formally apologise for hitting the princess of Arendelle with my horse," said Hans.

"No, no, no. It's fine. I'm not that princess. I mean, if you'd hit my sister, Elsa, it would be *yeesh*," Anna explained. "But lucky you – it's just me."

"Just you?" asked the prince.

Again they gazed at each other, until Anna was woken, as if from a spell, by the sound of bells.

"The bells! The coronation!" she said. "I better go. Uh... bye!"

After the coronation ceremony, Anna and Elsa stood together in the ballroom.

"Hi," said Elsa quietly. "You look beautiful."

"Thank you," Anna replied. "You look beautiful-ler."

"So, this is what a party looks like," said Elsa.

"This is so nice. I wish it could be like this all the time."

"Me too," said Elsa. "But it can't."

"Why not?" asked Anna.

"It just can't," insisted Elsa, turning away.

Holding back her tears, Anna made her way across the ballroom, where she found Hans. They began to dance together, swirling in time to the music. They talked, they laughed, and then wandered out into the gardens.

"Okay, wait, wait so you have *how* many brothers?" Anna asked Hans.

"Twelve older brothers. Three of them pretended I was invisible. Literally. For two years," Hans replied. "It's what brothers do."

"And sisters! Elsa and I were really close when we were little," Anna told him. "But then, one day, she just shut me out and I never knew why."

"I would never shut you out," promised Hans, taking hold of her hand.

That evening, Anna and Hans gazed at shooting stars and danced down the castle corridors.

"Can I say something crazy?" asked Hans. "Will you marry me?"

"Can I say something even crazier?" asked Anna. "Yes!"

They hurried back to the ballroom to find Elsa. "We would like… your blessing… of our marriage," they said together.

"Marriage?" gasped Elsa. "You can't marry a man you've just met."

"You can if it's true love," said Anna.

"Anna, what do you know about true love?"

"More than you! All you know is how to shut people out."

"You asked for my blessing, but my answer is no," said Elsa. "The party is over. Close the gates."

Anna tried to take Elsa's hand, but only managed to grab her glove. "Elsa, please. Please, I can't live like this anymore."

"Then leave," said Elsa, striding away.

"Why do you shut me out? Why do you shut the world out? What are you so afraid of?" Anna called across the ballroom.

"I said enough!" Elsa could no longer contain her powers. With a movement of her hand, dazzling shards of ice rose up into a fierce wall of icicle spikes.

"Sorcery!" cried the Duke of Weselton.

Elsa turned and fled, the Duke and his men hurrying after her.

"Please, just stay away from me," said Elsa. Then, without meaning to, she turned the castle steps to ice. The Duke slipped and fell.

"Monster!" he cried.

The crowds were looking at Elsa now with fear. She ran on, her footsteps creating an icy path across the fjord. By the time she reached the other side, the water had frozen. Thick snow fell from the sky.

"It's snowing! The queen has cursed this land," cried the Duke.

"It was an accident," said Anna. "She was scared. She didn't mean it. She didn't mean any of this. Tonight was my fault. I pushed her, so I'm the one that needs to go after her." She mounted her horse. "I leave Prince Hans in charge," she announced, then galloped after her sister.

High on the mountain slopes, Elsa removed her other glove and flung it away. Then, for the first time in a long time, she let her powers flow. She made ice crystals and a snowman, beautiful swirling clouds of snowflakes and icicle stairs to cross a mountain pass. On the snowy peak, she created a dazzling palace from gleaming ice. It rose up into the sky, its shards reaching for the clouds.

Far below her, Anna was struggling through thick snow. Her horse had bolted, and she was alone on the freezing mountain.

Then, ahead, she saw smoke pluming from the chimney of a little mountain shop. She hurried towards it, pushed open the door, and stepped inside.

"I was just wondering," said Anna as she gathered some winter supplies, "has another young woman – the queen, perhaps – passed through here?"

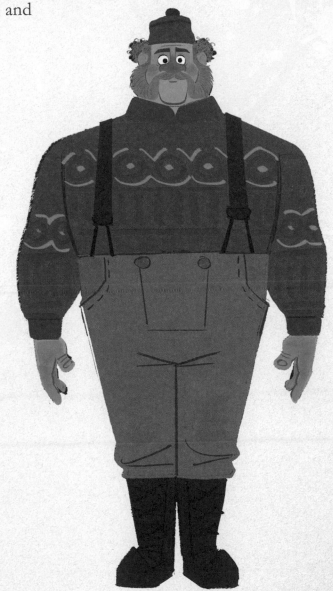

"Only one crazy enough to be out in this storm is you, dear," said the shopkeeper, Oaken. Then the door opened and a man entered, covered in snow. "You and this fellow."

The snow-covered man approached Anna. "Carrots," he said sternly. "Behind you."

"Oh, right. Excuse me," she said, moving out of the way.

"A real howler in July, yes? Wherever could it be coming from?" Oaken asked.

"The North Mountain," the man, Kristoff, replied.

Anna watched as Kristoff selected his supplies. Outside she could see his sled, piled high with blocks of ice. He must be an ice-seller, she realised. He must know the mountains. Perhaps he could help her find Elsa. Soon, though, Kristoff got into an argument with Oaken – who threw him out into the snow.

Anna followed him out to a little shed where he'd taken shelter with his reindeer, Sven.

"I want you to take me up the North Mountain," she said. "Look, I know how to stop this winter."

In exchange for supplies, and carrots for Sven, Kristoff agreed.

The sled dashed up the mountainside, Sven galloping hard.

"So tell me," said Kristoff, "what made the queen go all ice-crazy?"

"Oh, well, it was all my fault," Anna replied. She explained about Hans, her engagement, Elsa's reaction…

"Didn't your parents ever warn you about strangers?" Kristoff asked, shocked at her hasty engagement.

"Yes, they did. But Hans is not a stranger," said Anna. "It doesn't matter. It's true love."

Suddenly, Kristoff stopped the sled. He held up his lantern and peered into the darkness. Behind them, he saw glowing yellow eyes.

"Sven, go. Go!" yelled Kristoff, urging on his reindeer.

"What are they?" asked Anna.

"Wolves," said Kristoff.

Faster and faster they went, the wolves drawing nearer, leaping at them, snapping and snarling.

They outran the wolves, but ahead was a looming precipice.

"Jump, Sven!" Kristoff yelled.

Anna, Kristoff and Sven flew through the air, crash-landing on the snowy slopes beyond as Kristoff's sled burst into flames below.

"I'll replace your sled and everything in it," promised Anna. "And I understand if you don't want to help me anymore."

Then she continued up the mountain, alone.

Kristoff watched as Anna turned one way, then another, and then tripped. "Hold up!" he said, sighing. "We're coming."

"You are?" asked Anna excitedly. "I mean, sure. I'll let you tag along."

❄· ·❄·· ·❄

As the sun rose, they gazed back down the mountain. There lay Arendelle, frozen by Elsa's magic.

Ahead, the trees sparkled with frozen raindrops. "I never knew winter could be so beautiful," said Anna.

"But it's so white," said a voice. "You know, how about a little colour?"

Anna and Kristoff looked down and gasped. Between them stood a snowman. A walking, talking snowman.

"Hi, everyone. I'm Olaf. And I like warm hugs."

"Olaf!" said Anna, thinking back to her childhood. "Did Elsa build you?"

"Yeah. Why?"

"I'll tell you why," said Kristoff. "We need Elsa to bring back summer."

"Summer? Oh, I don't know why," said Olaf, "but I've always loved the idea of summer, and sun, and all things hot."

"Really? I'm guessing you don't have much experience with heat," said Kristoff.

"Nope!" Olaf replied. "So come on! Elsa's this way. Let's go bring back summer!"

He set off, leading them up the mountain.

Kristoff paused for a moment. "Somebody's gotta tell him."

When they finally reached the ice palace, Anna told the others to wait outside. Then she opened the door and crossed the glittering ice hall.

"Elsa," she called, "it's me, Anna."

Looking up, she saw her sister on the floor above, dazzling in her sparkling gown.

"Woah, Elsa, you look different. It's a good different. And this place, it's amazing."

"Thank you," said Elsa. "I never knew what I was capable of."

"I'm so sorry about what happened. If I'd have known—" said Anna.

"No, no, no, it's okay. You don't have to apologise. But you should probably go. Please," Elsa said. "You belong down in Arendelle."

"So do you."

"No, Anna, I belong here. Alone. Where I can be who I am without hurting anybody."

Before Anna could say anything more, Olaf ran in.

"Olaf?" said Elsa, gazing at him.

"He's just like the one we built as kids," Anna reminded her. "Elsa, we were so close. We can be like that again."

Then, as gently as she could, she told Elsa about the eternal winter she had left behind. She pleaded with her to bring back summer, but Elsa didn't know how.

Worry mounted inside Elsa like a swirling blizzard. Then, without meaning to… she struck Anna in the heart with her magic.

Kristoff entered the palace just as Anna fell. "Anna, are you okay?" he asked, rushing to her side.

"I'm okay. I'm fine," said Anna, masking her pain. She looked at her sister. "I'm not leaving without you, Elsa."

"Yes, you are," Elsa said. Then she created a giant, menacing snowman who hurled them from the palace.

Outside, on the snowy slopes, Anna despaired. "I can't go back to Arendelle with the weather like this."

But Kristoff was more worried about Anna. More of her hair was turning white. "It's because she struck you, isn't it? Anna, you need help, okay? Come on!"

"Where are we going?" asked Olaf.

"To see my friends," replied
Kristoff. "And don't worry,
they'll be able to fix this."

▪· — ·▪·▪ — ·▪

It was a long journey. By
the time they drew near,
darkness had fallen.

"So, about my friends,"
Kristoff explained to Anna.
"Well, I say friends… they're
more like family. They can
be a little… inappropriate.
And loud. Very loud."

"Kristoff, they sound
wonderful," said Anna.

Finally, they arrived at a clearing ringed by boulders. "Okay, then, meet my family!" Kristoff announced. He started greeting the boulders.

"They're rocks," Anna whispered to Olaf.

"He's crazy," Olaf whispered back. "I'll distract him while you run."

"Uh, okay," said Anna. "Well, I'm gonna go…"

But then the boulders began shaking. They sprang to life and that's when Anna realised… Kristoff's family were trolls.

"Kristoff's home!" they cheered.

"He's brought a girl," said one. "She'll do nicely for our Kristoff."

"That's not why I brought her here," replied Kristoff.

But before he could say more, Anna collapsed against him, her eyes closing.

"She's as cold as ice," Kristoff said.

Grand Pabbie rushed forward, taking Anna's hands in his. "Anna, your life is in danger," he said. "There is ice in your heart put there by your sister. If not removed, to solid ice will you freeze, forever."

"But you can remove it, right?" asked Kristoff.

"I cannot," said Grand Pabbie. "If it was her head, that would be easy. But only an act of true love can thaw a frozen heart."

"A true love's kiss, perhaps?" suggested one of the trolls.

"Anna," said Kristoff urgently, "we've got to get you back to Hans."

At that moment, however, Hans and a small band of men had reached Elsa's ice palace. Anna's horse had returned without her, and sensing she was in trouble, Hans had set out to find her.

Battling past the snow monster, they spotted Elsa at the palace gates.

"Stay away!" begged Elsa, forced to defend herself against their crossbows.

"Queen Elsa," called Hans, "don't be the monster they fear you are."

Elsa heard his words, her anger fading fast. As she lowered her arms, one of the Duke's men took aim. Hans ran at him, sending his crossbow bolt soaring to the ceiling, where it cut loose an icicle chandelier. It fell down toward Elsa, knocking her unconscious.

When Elsa woke, she was in a tiny cell in Arendelle, her hands bound by chains. Gazing out the window, she saw the frozen fjord. "What have I done?" she whispered.

Behind her, the door unlocked and Hans entered.

"Why did you bring me here?" demanded Elsa. "I'm a danger to Arendelle. Get Anna."

"Anna has not returned," replied Hans. "If you would just stop the winter. Bring back summer, please."

"Don't you see?" said Elsa. "I can't. You have to tell them to let me go."

"I will do what I can," promised Hans, locking the door behind him.

At the castle gates, Kristoff handed Anna to the servants. "Get her warm," he instructed. "And find Prince Hans immediately."

They took Anna straight to Hans. She stumbled into his arms.

"What happened out there?" he asked, carrying her to a chair near the fireplace.

"Elsa struck me with her powers," she explained. "She froze my heart, and only an act of true love can save me."

"A true love's kiss," Hans said. He bent as if to kiss her… then stopped. "Oh, Anna. If only there was someone out there who loved you."

"What? You said you did." Anna shivered with disbelief.

"As thirteenth in line in my own kingdom, I didn't stand a chance… I knew I'd have to marry into the throne somewhere," Hans explained. "You were so desperate for love. You were willing to marry me just like that."

He began to pour water over the fire, slowly extinguishing it. "All that's left now is to kill Elsa and bring back summer."

"You won't get away with this," whispered Anna, too weak to move.

Prince Hans strode over to the door. "Oh, I already have," he said, locking the door behind him and trapping Anna in the freezing room.

In the great dining hall, Prince Hans announced Anna's death.

"At least we got to say our marriage vows… before she died in my arms," he said despairingly. "With a heavy heart, I charge Queen Elsa of Arendelle with treason, and sentence her to death."

In the library, Anna lay shivering on the floor, watching ice spread across the ceiling.

She saw the door unlock, and Olaf pattered inside. He rushed straight to the fire and relit it.

"So, where's Hans?" he asked, confused.

"I was wrong about him. It wasn't true love," said Anna. "I don't even know what love is."

"Love," said Olaf, "is putting someone else's needs before yours, like… you know, how Kristoff brought you back here to Hans."

"Kristoff loves me?"

"Wow, you really don't know anything about love, do you?" Then his face began to droop.

"Olaf, you're melting!" said Anna.

"Some people are worth melting for," he said… then panicked. "Just maybe not right this second!"

As he spoke, a window burst open, and Olaf hurried over to close it. Looking out, he saw Kristoff, on Sven's back, galloping towards the castle for Anna.

"There's your act of true love, right there, riding across the fjords like a valiant, pungent reindeer king… Come on!"

They hurried outside. Growing weaker by the minute, Anna struggled through the blizzard. She knew she didn't have much time. "Kristoff!" she called.

As Anna struggled to reach Kristoff, Elsa had broken free from her cell and was standing on the icy fjord.

"Elsa," said Hans, approaching her through the swirling storm, "you can't run from this! Your sister is dead because of you."

In despair, Elsa dropped to her knees. At once the storm stilled, halted by her grief. As the blizzard cleared, Kristoff and Anna finally found each other.

But then Anna saw Hans, his sword raised, ready to strike her sister...

For a moment, Anna looked longingly at Kristoff. Then she ran, throwing herself between Elsa and Hans's sword.

At that same instant, her body turned to ice.

Hans struck her. His sword splintered into a hundred pieces, and he was sent flying backwards onto the ground.

Elsa flung her arms around the icy statue of her sister. "Anna, no, no, please no," she sobbed.

Kristoff, Sven, and Olaf all looked on, desolate. The watching crowds bowed their heads.

But then, as if by magic, Anna began to thaw; her eyes opened. "Oh, Elsa," she whispered.

"You sacrificed yourself for me?" said Elsa.

"I love you," Anna replied.

"An act of true love will thaw a frozen heart!" Olaf exclaimed.

"Love… of course," said Elsa. She spread her hands, and Arendelle, too, began to thaw. The waters of the fjord lapped the shore, the castle fountains began to flow, and flowers showed their colour once more.

"I knew you could do it," said Anna.

"Hands down, this is the best day of my life," said Olaf as he began to melt. "And quite possibly the last."

"Olaf! Hang on, little guy," said Elsa. She created a snow cloud over his head to keep him safe.

"My own personal flurry," giggled Olaf.

Beside them, Hans struggled to his feet. "Anna?" he said, a puzzled frown on his face. "But she froze your heart."

"The only frozen heart around here is yours," replied Anna. Then she punched him.

⬩⬩ ⬩⬩⬩⬩ ⬩⬩

With the ice gone, the ships in Arendelle's harbour could set sail once more. Prince Hans was taken back to his country, never to return.

Down by the waterfront, Anna was showing Kristoff his new sled.

"I can't accept this," said Kristoff.

"Do you like it?" Anna asked.

"Like it? I love it!" said Kristoff, twirling her through the air.

"I could kiss you," said Kristoff. "I could. I mean, I'd like to," he added bashfully. "I'd… May I? We me. I mean, may we?"

"We may," said Anna, smiling. Then, she kissed him.

✦ ✦✦ ✦

Over by the castle courtyard, the people of Arendelle were skating on a magical ice rink that Elsa had created.

"I like the open gates," said Anna, joining her sister.

"We are never closing them again," Elsa replied, and with a wave of her hand, she gave Anna a pair of sparkling skates.

"Oh, Elsa, they're beautiful, but you know I don't ska—"

"Come on! You can do it," said Elsa, taking her sister's hands.

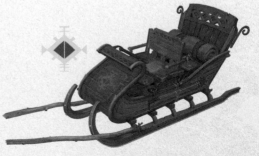

And they swirled across the ice, their world full of laughter and magic, two sisters together again at last.

And they lived

happily ever after... for now.

The End

The Art of Disney Frozen

In 1937, the Disney Studios began development on a biography of the author Hans Christian Andersen. Animated sequences were to be based on works including *The Little Mermaid* and *The Snow Queen*. The project was shelved in 1942. In the 1990s and early 2000s, there were various attempts to revisit the project, but it wasn't until 2008 that the film we now know as *Frozen* began to take shape. Under the directorship of Chris Buck and Jennifer Lee, and the art direction of Michael Giaimo, the style of the film was inspired by the hand-drawn classics of the 1950s, Little Golden Books, and Scandinavian design. Animators and special effects artists took research field trips, visiting Jackson Hole, Wyoming, to experience walking, running and falling in deep snow. The lighting team visited an ice hotel, to study how light refracts and reflects on ice and snow, and a number of artists visited Norway, drawing inspiration from its scenery and culture. It is estimated that around 600-650 people worked on *Frozen*, including seventy-plus animators. Throughout this book you can see concept art, costume design and more from the following Walt Disney Animation Studios artists.

David Womersley

London-born David Womersley joined the Walt Disney Studios in 1996 to supervise Disney's first CGI Layout Department on the film *Dinosaur*. He has worked as a designer and visual development artist on Disney animated films including *Bolt*, *Tangled*, *Wreck-It Ralph*, *Frozen*, and, most recently, *Frozen 2*.
Concept art on pages 2-3, 7, 8 and 70-71.

Cory Loftis

Joining the Walt Disney Animation Studios in 2011, Cory Loftis has worked as a character designer and visual development artist for films such as *Wreck-It Ralph*, *Frozen*, *Zootopia*, and *Ralph Breaks the Internet*. Loftis specialises in creating concept designs and facial expression sheets for characters. He is currently serving as production designer on Disney's upcoming 2020 animated feature release.
Concept art on pages 4, 23, 24, 25, 33, 43, 50, 59 and 62.

Brittney Lee

After seeing *The Little Mermaid* as a child, Brittney Lee decided to pursue a career in animation. Lee is a visual development artist at the Walt Disney Animation Studios and has worked on the Disney short *Paperman* as well as *Wreck-It Ralph* and *Frozen*. For *Frozen*, Lee designed all of Anna's dresses and hairstyles in addition to contributing to the design of Elsa's hair, Elsa's iconic dress and the rosemaling on the backgrounds. She also recently contributed to the look of *Frozen 2* and illustrated the children's book *Mary Blair's Unique Flair: The Girl Who Became One of the Disney Legends*.
Concept art on pages 10, 19 and 40.

Bill Schwab

Bill Schwab joined Walt Disney Animation Studios in 2006 as a character designer on *The Princess and the Frog* and has worked on films including *Wreck-It Ralph*, *Tangled*, *Frozen* and *Moana*. For *Frozen*, Schwab took on the role of lead character designer and design supervisor. For *Frozen 2*, he served as art director, characters, and is currently working in a similar capacity for Disney's 2021 animated feature release.
Concept art on pages 11, 20, 21, 22, 31, 35, 38, 41, 45, 48 (lower left), 49, 54, 56, 57 and 61.

Fawn Veerasunthorn

Growing up in Thailand, Fawn Veerasunthorn's interest in animation was inspired by *Dumbo*, the Disney film about a little flying elephant. At age nineteen, Veerasunthorn moved to the United States to study animation, and she joined the Walt Disney Animation Studios in 2011 as a story artist. She has contributed to many Disney animated films, including *Zootopia*, *Frozen* and *Moana*. Most recently, she served as story supervisor on *Ralph Breaks the Internet*.
Storyboard on pages 12 and 26.

Marc Smith

Born and raised in Southern California, Marc Smith developed an interest in art and animation at an early age, and remembers being influenced by such Disney classics as *Dumbo*. From 1991 through 1993, he pursued his creative interests at California Institute of the Arts, which led to a starting level job in 1993 as an in-betweener trainee on *The Lion King*. Smith went on to animate *Rhapsody in Blue* featured in *Fantasia/2000*, the adult title character in *Hercules*, Kerchak in *Tarzan*, Kuzco and Kuzco Llama in *The Emperor's New Groove*, and John Silver in *Treasure Planet*, among others. For Tangled, he made the switch to story, and has gone on to work in that capacity on *Frozen*, as well as *Big Hero 6* and *Zootopia* as lead story artist and *Frozen 2* as director of story.
Storyboard on page 12.

Paul Briggs

Joining the Walt Disney Studios as an intern in 1997, Paul Briggs began his career as a visual effects artist on *Hercules*. Briggs has also contributed to many Disney animated films as a story artist and has even lent his voice to a few roles. For *Frozen*, Briggs worked as a story artist and was also the voice of Marshmallow. He is currently directing, with Dean Wellins, Disney's 2020 animated feature release.
Storyboard on page 12; story sketch on page 46.

James Finch

James Finch joined the Walt Disney Studios in 1994 as an intern. Since then he has worked in various roles, from layout artist and visual development artist to production designer on films such as *Tarzan*, *The Princess and the Frog*, *Frozen*, *Frozen 2*, and several upcoming short films and feature projects.
Concept art on pages 13 and 47.

Dale Baer

Joining the Walt Disney Studios in the 1970s as part of a new talent development program, Dale Baer has worked as a character animator, supervising animator and visual development artist on some of the biggest Disney films of the last forty years, including *Robin Hood*, *The Lion King*, *Frozen* and *Zootopia*. Baer has also been the recipient of the Annie Award for his character animation of Yzma in *The Emperor's New Groove* and the Winsor McCay Award for his contributions to the art of animation. He retired from Disney in 2015.
Story sketch on page 14.

Normand Lemay

French-Canadian Normand Lemay moved to Los Angeles in 2009 to join the Walt Disney Animation Studios. Lemay has worked as a story artist on films including *Frozen*, *Big Hero 6*, *Zootopia*, *Moana* and *Ralph Breaks the Internet*. His most recent credit is head of story on *Frozen 2*.
Storyboard on page 15.

John Ripa

John Ripa is an animator, story artist and head of story at the Walt Disney Animation Studios. Ripa animated the titular character in *Pocahontas*, Quasimodo in *The Hunchback of Notre Dame* and was supervising animator on Jim Hawkins in *Treasure Planet*. He has also contributed to Disney animated films, including *Tangled*, *Frozen* and *Moana*. For *Frozen*, Ripa developed story sketches of Elsa while watching the voice actor, Idina Menzel, sing in the studio. He is currently serving as head of story on Disney's 2020 animated feature release.
Storyboard on pages 16, 17 and 27.

Jim Finn

Jim Finn has worked as a background stylist, matte painter and visual development artist on a wide variety of Disney animated films such as *101 Dalmatians 2: Patch's London Adventure*, *The Jungle Book 2*, *Bolt*, *Frozen*, *Big Hero 6*, *Moana* and *Frozen 2*. In addition to his continuing visual development role on feature films, he recently art directed four upcoming short films created as part of Walt Disney Animation Studios' "Short Circuit" programme.
Concept art on pages 18 and 34.

Jean Gillmore

Joining Disney in the early 1990s, Jean Gillmore worked as a character designer, eventually specialising in costume design on some of Disney and Pixar's biggest animated features of the 1990s and 2000s. Gillmore has worked on character design for films including *Aladdin*, *Pocahontas*, *Toy Story* and *Mulan*. Notably, she worked on Frozen as a visual development artist, helping to create the sumptuous and iconic costumes of the 2013 hit. She served in a similar capacity on *Frozen 2*.
Concept art on page 28 (right).

Shiyoon Kim

Shiyoon Kim is a character designer working at the Walt Disney Animation Studios and has contributed to films including *Tangled*, *Winnie the Pooh*, *Wreck-It Ralph* and *Frozen*, for which he was the character designer for the Duke of Weselton. In 2014, Kim was the lead character designer for *Big Hero 6* and created the looks of Hiro, Tadashi Hamada and Go Go Tomago. Among his recent non-Disney credits was a stint as character designer on the 2018 feature *Spider-Man: Into the Spider-Verse*. His most recent Disney credit is on the Studio's 2020 animated feature release.
Story sketch on page 28 (left).

Dan Lund

Starting out as a production assistant, Dan Lund joined the Walt Disney Studios in the early 1990s. Learning on the job, he developed his skills and now works as a visual effects animator. Lund has worked across many Disney animated films, including *Beauty and the Beast*, *Hercules*, *The Princess and the Frog* and *Frozen*. For *Frozen*, Lund created the ice, fire, wind and dress transformations. His most recent credits include creative lead on the 'Frozen Ever After' attraction at Epcot and the hit Broadway version of *Frozen*, as well as effects designer on *Frozen 2*.
Concept art on page 29.

Scott Watanabe

Scott Watanabe joined the Walt Disney Animation Studios as a trainee, working on *Tangled*. He now works as a visual development artist and has contributed to films such as *Wreck-It Ralph*, *Frozen*, *Zootopia* and *Ralph Breaks the Internet*. His Disney credits also include *Big Hero 6*, for which he served as art director. Most recently, he has helped to define the look of Disney's 2020 animated feature release and several experimental short films for the Studio.
Concept art on page 30.

Minkyu Lee

Minkyu Lee is a writer and animator who has created visual development art for Disney films such as *Wreck-It Ralph*, *Frozen*, *Big Hero 6* and *Moana*. A short film he directed, *Adam and Dog*, received an Oscar nomination in 2013 for Best Animated Short Film, and went on to win an Annie Award for Best Animated Short Subject.
Concept art on pages 32, 48 and 53.

Jin Kim

Born in South Korea, Jin Kim joined the Walt Disney Studios in 1995. Kim specialises in character design, concept design and facial expression sheets for characters. Kim has worked on films such as *Hercules*, *Tarzan*, *The Emperor's New Groove*, *Tangled*, *Zootopia*, *Frozen* and *Frozen 2*.
Concept art on pages 36, 44 and 52.

Lisa Keene

Joining the Walt Disney Studios in 1982, Lisa Keene has worked as a visual development artist and background supervisor on some of Disney's most beloved films, including *Beauty and the Beast*, *The Lion King*, *Enchanted*, *The Princess and the Frog* and *Tangled*. Most recently, she served as co-production designer for *Frozen 2*.
Concept art on pages 37, 51, 60 and 63; colour key on page 55.

Michael Giaimo

A Cal Arts graduate, Michael Giaimo began his career at the Walt Disney Studios in the 1970s, first in-betweening on production before moving into story development. Giaimo's early career saw him working on films such as *The Fox and the Hound* and *The Black Cauldron*. After a short break from the Walt Disney Studios, Giaimo returned, serving as the art director for *Pocahontas*. For *Frozen*, Giaimo once again took on the role of art director. In his role as production designer for *Frozen 2*, he has helped to create some inspired new locations, costumes and artistic fantasy that elevates the film to new cinematic heights.
Concept art on page 39.

Julia Kalantarova

Born in Uzbekistan, Julia Kalantarova joined the Walt Disney Animation Studios to work on the visual development of *Frozen*. Kalantarova created concept art for the hit 2013 film. Julia had numerous credits on a variety of popular television animated shows, including *Bob's Burgers*. She passed away in 2016 at the age of forty-five following a battle with breast cancer.
Concept art on page 42.

Hyun-min Lee

South Korean animator Hyun-min Lee moved to the United States in 2000 to study painting and animation. After training with legendary Disney animator Eric Goldberg, Lee joined Disney's animation department and has worked on such major hits as *The Princess and the Frog*, *Wreck-It Ralph* and *Frozen*. Her most recent credit is on *Frozen 2* as animation supervisor.
Concept art on page 58.

❄ Glossary ❄

Colour key: establishes the look and feel of a background painting and the overall colour of a scene, helping animators avoid any colour overlaps or clashes when placing characters and objects on backgrounds.

Concept art: drawings, paintings or sketches prepared in the early stages of a film's development, which are often used to inspire the staging, mood and atmosphere of scenes.

Story sketch: a drawing or digital creation that indicates a particular moment in a story. These are usually arranged in order with other sketches to help work out the story in detail.

Storyboard: a large board on which story sketches are pinned, showing the action of a sequence.